NOT MY FIGHT

The Art of Preserving Your Peace

L.A. Owens

Not My Fight
The Art of Preserving Peace

Copyright © 2024. L.A. Owens (All rights reserved)

Printed in the United States of America. No part of this book may be used or reproduced, stored in a retrieval system, or transmitted in any way by any means – electronic, mechanical, photocopy, or otherwise – without the prior permissions of the copyright holder, except by reviewer who may quote brief passages in a review to be printed in magazine newspaper or by radio/ TV announcement, as provided by USA copyright law. The author and the publisher will not be held responsible for any errors within the manuscript. All characters appearing in this work are fictitious. Any resemblance to real persons, living or dead, is purely coincidental.
www.laowens.com

Scriptures are taken from the KING JAMES VERSION (KJV): KING JAMES VERSION, public domain.

First Edition
ISBN: 978-0-9964713-4-3
Category: Motivational / Inspirational / Empowerment / Self-Help / Family

Editor: Marni Macrae
Cover Art/Design: Rebecacovers
Author Photography: LaTonya Irving (livingirving.com)
Author Photography: Indra Rogers (Indraphotography.com)
Book Interior Formatting & Layout Designer: Accuracy4sure

Contents

Preface iv

Introduction 1

Decision 3

Draw 6

Combination 9

On the Ropes 13

Clinch 19

Bob and Weave 29

Jab 33

Cross 37

Blocking 40

Knockout 44

Foul 47

Below the Belt 56

Footwork 62

The Author 70

Acknowledgments 72

Preface

Not My Fight: The Art of Preserving Peace resonates with the spirit of a disciplined fighter in the world of boxing. Imagine being in the ring, skilled and ready but wise enough to know that not every punch needs to be thrown. It's about discerning which battles are worth fighting and which are better left alone. A seasoned veteran understands that energy should be conserved for the matches that truly matter. By focusing on their own game plan and not getting drawn into unnecessary brawls, they maintain their strength and clarity. *Embrace this wisdom in life*—know when to step back, preserve your peace, and channel your energy into fights that are genuinely yours.

The path to self-care is like training for the ring. It starts by shedding old behaviors and patterns that no longer serve you, much like an athlete refining their technique. To evolve into the finest version of yourself, you may need to shut doors that don't contribute to your well-being, just as a champion avoids distractions to focus on maintaining their belt. Your life's journey is yours alone, and seeking peace within it is essential.

When faced with disrespect, create distance. And when miscommunication arises, take a moment to reflect, just as a fighter reassesses their strategy between rounds.

Peace often comes when you forge your own path, finding your unique rhythm. It's like dancing to your own beat, connecting deeply with what truly aligns within your soul. The *best* battles are those where you feel confident in victory even before the final bell rings.

There's an art to maintaining peace in your life, and it is my hope that this book serves as a guide by sharing the experiences that have taught me how to preserve my own peace. Choose your battles with care, and remember, it's Not My Fight—some conflicts are deeply entrenched, extending far beyond our influence.

*Even in the midst of destruction,
a flower can still bloom*

Introduction

Life isn't perfect, but sometimes everything aligns beautifully with the current season. Currently, I'm embarking on a personal journey that's all about deep self-discovery and unwavering dedication to my well-being. Embracing this path, I'm learning more about *who I am*, *what I need*, and *how to nurture* myself each day. It's a continuous process of figuring out what truly matters and finding authentic ways to enrich my life. Each step I take is another page in the story of becoming the best version of myself, filled with moments of growth and an ever-expanding understanding of my own *needs* and *desires*. This journey is not just about surviving but thriving, finding balance, and cultivating a life that feels truly fulfilling and genuine.

Today, I understand that it's my responsibility to stay true to myself. Either I'll fit into others' lives or I won't. My biggest mistake was trying to force a fit where there wasn't one. The heartaches that took years to heal have taught me to let things happen organically, rather than forcing them. It's in those forced moments that I risk losing my peace—a price far too great to pay. No gain is worth sacrificing my peace! I've invested so much in myself already, and I owe it to myself to protect that.

Living authentically and safeguarding my well-being is my top priority, and nothing is worth compromising that.

I've realized that going up against hidden agendas, deceit, manipulation, jealousy, false friendships, and others' insecurities is like stepping into a boxing ring with an opponent who never quits. It's utterly exhausting and draining and is "*Not My Fight!*"

I've learned that these battles no longer deserve a place in my life. By stepping out of that toxic ring, I've found my peace. I can now chase after what genuinely enriches my life with unstoppable enthusiasm.

Hindsight is always 20/20, isn't it? If I had the knowledge back then that I do now, I would have avoided those draining battles altogether. They almost drove me to the brink of losing my sanity. But now that I've found my inner peace, I can direct my energy into becoming the ultimate, unbothered version of myself. It wasn't easy, and the path was filled with obstacles and challenges, but I had to learn the hard way that not every battle is worth fighting, and some are best left alone.

The heartaches and struggles I faced have forged me into the person I am today. They taught me the importance of *letting go* of what doesn't serve me and focusing on what truly matters—prioritizing my *mental* and *emotional* health above all else.

My story is a tale of triumph over adversity, and I'm excited to share it with you. It's the realization that true happiness comes from *within*.

So, let's dive into the journey that led me here.

Decision

In the world of boxing, when all three judges reach a consensus on who the winner of the match is, it culminates in what's known as a unanimous *decision*. It's the ultimate affirmation of a boxer's performance in the ring.

Judges might hand out scores and opinions, but in *life*, we're often left to figure things out without a roadmap. Making decisions solo can be pretty nerve-wracking, but they shape us in surprising ways. Life is a quest of self-discovery, where sometimes you just have to take a leap of faith. *Every choice*, no matter how difficult, weaves into the tapestry of your unique story, shaping who you are and guiding your path forward.

Life, for me, has indeed been a quest. My search for "home" felt like a never-ending journey, it wasn't just about having a roof over my head, it was about discovering a place where I felt *love*, *peace*, and *belonging*. With every step, I pursued a sanctuary of *calm* and *solitude*. Like a boxer facing relentless punches and challenges, I never gave up. I kept moving forward, always believing that I would recognize it when I finally found it.

Life's journey for peace and belonging can take us to unexpected places. For a time, I believed my sanctuary was that luxurious house that my ex-spouse and I owned in a prestigious, guarded, gated, golf community. *It wasn't.*

I sought solace in marriages and relationships, hoping to find that ultimate haven. *It wasn't there either.* Yet, in the stillness of a deep dream, the real truth revealed itself. They say 'home is where the heart is,' but God showed me that my true *home* wasn't in any place or in companionship but in the love that I found in my child. I had indeed discovered my sanctuary, not once but twice.

The instant I first saw my son, and every time since—when our eyes meet, when we share a kiss, a touch, a hug, or a smile—he embodies *home*. In his presence, I find an unparalleled contentment, a sense that all is right in my world. He is a reflection of me, a continuation of my being. His features mirror mine; his mannerisms echo my own, and in him, I see both the good and challenging traits that are unmistakably me.

I found something precious and then lost it due to poor decisions, placing too much trust in the capabilities of others over my own. The initial mistake was entrusting my son's upbringing to his father following our acrimonious divorce. It wasn't that I felt he was incapable of raising him, I just didn't recognize how much my son still needed his mother's nurturing. With every fiber of my being, I truly believed I was making the best choice for him.

Subsequently, I realized that my decision had unintended consequences. The absence of my daily presence created a void that no one else could fill. My son's need for my nurturing touch, guidance, and emotional support became painfully apparent. I was so focused on what I thought was best for him that I overlooked the essential role I played in his life.

The weight of this decision haunted me intensely, lingering in my thoughts and emotions. It was a heavy burden to bear, knowing that my choice would have far-reaching consequences. It was a painful lesson that etched itself into my heart and mind. However, it taught me the profound importance of being **present**. It was a stark reminder of the irreplaceable role a mother plays in her child's life. This realization, though gained through immense pain, underscored just how significant my presence and dedication truly are. It wasn't his fight. It was *my* fight!

The experience strengthened my resolve to support my son in every conceivable manner. The emotional impact and determination to learn from not being present every day rendered each moment significantly more meaningful, particularly in anticipation of this forthcoming life-changing event. I needed to consider everything my son had endured. The decision before me was crucial—it required deep reflection on "my child, whom I brought into this world." I couldn't make this choice without putting him first! Yet I hadn't foreseen the intense heartache that would come from losing something I never realized was essential to my being…

Draw

The weight of this decision pressed heavily on my heart, knowing it would affect both my son and I significantly. The pain was unexpected, a stark realization of our deep bond and the importance of what was lost, *another child*. It's safe to say that this decision took me to the depths of *hell* and back. The pain and the screams are etched in my memory as if they happened just yesterday. I will never, ever forget that dreadful day.

The heartbeat.

The formation.

It all felt so hauntingly real; *hell*, that is.

It's a moment that will forever be seared into my soul, a haunting reminder of the immense impact of that decision on that day. The emotional anguish I experienced was overwhelming, a torment of sorrow and regret that threatened to engulf me entirely.

This was *my fight*, *my battle*, and *my pain*. And despite everything, I faced it with the hope that one day, I would find peace within myself. That day has yet to come for the decision that I made on that day.

It felt as though the nurse was an angel sent to ensure my decision was unanimous, silently asking, "Are you sure?" *I wasn't.*

It felt as though heaven itself was crying that day. My cries were inconsolable, my sobs coming from the deepest part of my being. I felt I had disappointed God in a way that words cannot begin to describe. God had given me *home* in my children, and I destroyed the most precious gift of all: *Life.*

I extinguished a part of my *own* being. The weight of that realization was overwhelming, a sorrow so profound it left an indelible mark on my soul. Even though I tried to convince myself that I had atoned for this act, the reality is that I still struggle with self-forgiveness.

Deep within my spirit, I felt that she was a girl—the daughter I never knew how much I needed until she was no longer. She symbolized my ultimate refuge, yet I destroyed the future we could have shared.

The absence of my unborn child left a void within me, a gaping emptiness that I couldn't fill. For years, I imagined her looks, the bond we might have had, and her age each birthday, until the sorrow grew too intense to bear. The pain of this decision has been a constant companion, a relentless reminder of what could have been.

Over time, I discovered tranquility by shifting my focus away from the *'what-ifs'* and the *'could haves'* or *'should haves.'* I ceased marking the birthdays, ceased searching for girls who might look like her. I had to halt everything for the sake of peace. Although I may never forgive myself, I find solace in the fact that I no longer torture myself with daydreams of what could never be.

Even now, in his thirties, my son makes no secret of his discontent with being an *only* child. The choice was mine; his father actually wanted more children. Back then, our marriage had been on shaky ground, and I was against bringing another child into that uncertainty. I didn't believe in having children just to keep a marriage together. It was a difficult choice, made with everyone's best interests at heart. At that time, in the context of my marriage, having another child was just not an option.

In reality, it was about preserving my sanity and finding *peace*. The future was uncertain; maybe a child could have brought newfound joy amidst the losses from consecutive tragedies. Being in my early twenties, I lacked the tools to make such impactful decisions for all our futures. I simply didn't have the capacity to navigate those challenges back then. I wasn't a skilled enough fighter to take on such a heavy weight. The burden was too great, and I felt utterly unprepared to face it. In that moment, I realized the limits of my own strength and the major impact of the choices I had to make. The weight of it all was overwhelming, a reminder that sometimes, even our hardest decisions can feel insurmountable. My decision—but 'Not My Fight!

I had to let go!

Combination

A barrage of emotions and revelations hitting one after another—a *combination*, that's exactly how it felt. The child that was no longer wasn't from my son's father but from a man I met long after my divorce, many years later. It was a whirlwind romance filled with poems, sweet nothings, and unforgettable bliss. The fleeting nature of that connection made the decision even more complex and emotionally charged.

I had suspected that his erratic behavior upon learning of my pregnancy hinted at something deeper, possibly *someone else*. Only recently, after years of no contact, did the truth emerge during a brief exchange that he now has *a daughter*. The revelation felt like a different punch—a left jab, a straight right, a left hook hitting me in various ways.

This revelation involves the same individual who once professed his undying love for me and spoke of marriage. What seemed like a fairytale romance was overshadowed by a regrettable decision that remains the most painful story of my life. There are no second chances, no opportunities to reclaim that moment in time. No apologies or attempts to rectify can alter the past. It's an irrevocable change that has reshaped who

I am in ways I may never fully understand. Yet I accept complete responsibility for my *own* actions.

Storms constantly gather in our lives, for with the good comes the bad. In my defense, we took precautions. In his error, he was aware the condom had broken. We were two adults engaged in an act that bore consequences, of which we were both fully cognizant.

I had this gut feeling something was off with him, but I couldn't put my finger on it. Even his *so-called* female friends dropped hints when he introduced me to them in New York. Despite that, I never said a word to him. Why? Because it was "Not My Fight!"

He knows the truth, whatever it may be. His guilt might stick with him just as mine does. I made the decision to have the procedure done here in Florida instead of flying to the upper east coast for him to accompany me. He ensured he sent enough funds to cover everything that needed to be taken care of. Thankfully, I had a friend to escort me and comfort me through this ordeal. Ironically, he could relate because he had been in our shoes with someone in college. Yet another friend, my dear sister, assured me that we could take care of this child and begged me not to go through with it. There are too many days where I wish I had listened to her.

There's nothing that he could *say* nor *do* that would bring our child back.

Absolutely nothing!

And yet the storm keeps brewing...

"*Hey, I'm just checking on you and the family to make sure you're okay,*" he said.

"Thanks for checking. We're doing as well as can be expected. It's been like living in a movie. I can't even begin to explain the devastation. Let's just say, I'm finally ready to leave waterfront living," I replied. *"I don't know what awaits me. My family in the St. Petersburg/Tampa Bay area can't leave because of downed trees and power lines,"* I continued. *"A Category 5 hurricane would've wiped us off the map!"* I exclaimed.

"If there's anything I can do, let me know," he offered.

Did I believe him? *Yes, I did.* He made an effort to call and check on me and my family, and that should count for something, right? My online presence is visible to the world, yet we've never met in person again since our situationship ended. *Not once.*

We once talked about meeting when he was traveling to Miami and another time during his visit to Tampa, but it never materialized. Honestly, I don't think either of us was too eager to meet the other.

For me, there's nothing more to say or do. I once believed I needed closure, but now I see I don't. The desire for it has faded. Yet whenever I hear from him, it revives memories of who he was and the painful chapter he signifies in my life. It's an invariably bittersweet blend of emotions.

Our short-lived romance was one for the books, but it was never worth the pain that followed. Revisiting those memories is a reminder of the lessons learned and the strength gained from moving past that period.

In the end, it's about preserving my peace and understanding that some doors need to be *permanently closed*. Life is filled with moments that teach us to value ourselves and set boundaries, ensuring we don't repeat the same mistakes.

For the sake of my peace, having survived the storm of losing my precious child to my own hands and both hurricanes Helene and Milton, I knew it was time to close this door permanently and seal it off from my world for good; this is *"The Art of Preserving Peace."*

On the Ropes

A hopeless situation. Defenseless, I fought tirelessly to the brink of collapse, only to find myself here... *On the ropes.*

Life had worn me down, leaving me exhausted and vulnerable. Yet even in the moment of despair, there was a spark of fight within me, a strength that refused to give up!

I decided it was time for introspection, to understand why these hurricanes were impacting me so profoundly. Why was I permitting them to disturb the tranquility I strive so diligently to preserve?

How could one truly prepare for something that you've never experienced in life before? I had to remind myself that I am human. No matter how much I play the superhero role in others' lives, in my own life, I have to stay true to who I am.

Sometimes, the same goes with loved ones who can be as unpredictable as the sea, pushing against our best efforts to support them, and today was overwhelming like a tsunami. *My son,* my pride and joy, stood his ground, refusing to move even as the hurricane neared. His reason? A sense of security, having weathered the last storm unscathed and believing that not being in a mandatory evacuation zone meant safety for his family. Yet this hurricane was being called the storm of the century. When meteorologists are visibly shaken, it's an unmistakable signal of the gravity of the threat.

As a mother to an adult son and him being a father, I had to honor his choices. After ending the call, I cried inconsolably, feeling completely helpless, powerless, and overwhelmed. The mere thought of harm coming to them was intolerable. I wept until I could cry no more. At that moment, I sensed a divine presence reassuring me.

"This battle is not yours. *Give it to Me*," God urged.

And so, I took a deep breath. I loosened my grip and opened my hands wide, entrusting the burden to God at that very moment.

I instantly felt peace.

In that moment, I realized *the gravity of the situation extended beyond just another storm menacing my cherished hometown.* Residing in an area known as 'paradise,' a magnet for global vacationers, had always been a source of happiness. However, I was becoming tired of this place I treasured so much. I once thought the allure of this endless holiday existence would persist, that I would forever bask in the opulence of living by the water—a dream come true. The liberty to roam the adjacent cities freely, partaking in any pursuit my heart fancied, had always seemed like a scene out of a movie. Today felt different.

I've lived here my whole life and have never witnessed flooding like what we saw a few weeks ago from hurricane Helene that didn't directly hit us, and now, just weeks later, we're facing another storm.

During the evacuation, I drove for hours in complete silence, observing the other cars as I passed by. Although I was physically present, my mind was elsewhere. I reflected on my beautiful grandchildren, their innocence and their abundant talents. Without realizing it, my emotions were intensifying. After a long journey, I arrived safely at my destination. Both emotionally and physically exhausted, I still had not fully processed the emotional toll of the experience.

I called my son's father multiple times, urging him to persuade our son to evacuate; it wasn't about money or not having a place to go. He felt secure because the last storm hadn't caused much damage. But in my humble opinion, that storm was incomparable to the one approaching. The previous storm had missed us, but this one was on a direct path to the Tampa Bay area.

We hunkered down as the storm hit the shore. Our hometown lay directly across the bridge from Tampa. We witnessed the transformation of one of America's top beaches, Clearwater Beach, turning into an unrecognizable landscape. Tragically, an elderly couple was found in their vehicle, unable to escape. Another individual was discovered beneath the sands, and boats were capsized in front yards, resembling a parade of boats. Homes were destroyed as electric vehicles ignited due to the saltwater, creating an endless series of disasters previously unheard of in our area.

For over a century, we had been fortunate. Whenever a storm was forecasted to strike Tampa directly, its course would unexpectedly shift, sparing the Tampa Bay area. Folklore attributed this to an indigenous prayer that shielded the land for a hundred years. But the storm approaching us now was unlike any other; it had a different, ominous feel. Surviving Hurricane Charley's direct hit on Orlando at ninety-five miles per hour was a serious ordeal. However, the impending storm seemed to instill an unprecedented level of fear; it sent our minds into a frenzy.

As I attempted to open my laptop and start some work after showering and settling in, the weight of everything overwhelmed me, and I found myself again sobbing uncontrollably. I had left behind relatives who were incredibly dear to me, and I felt powerless. Being hours away, there was nothing I could do for them. *How could this be happening? How could this be my life?*

Just the weekend before, I had spent a glorious day strolling along the beach, my long braids fluttering in the breeze, my feet splashing in the Atlantic Ocean, my favorite artists playing in my ears. I was in a state of awe; the water was my sanctuary of *calm*.

Now, mere days later, I found myself wondering if my family would be alright? Would I still have a home after the storm made landfall? The uncertainty was overwhelming. I had no control over anything, and that left me feeling incredibly uneasy. It saddened me deeply. My heart felt like a heavy burden. But once I let out that intense cry and declared, "*Lord, this is not my battle*," surrendering everything to God, I sensed relief on the horizon. I believed that God was taking this burden, lifting it from my shoulders, and holding it in His own.

Guided by faith, I shifted my perspective. From a distance, there was little I could do physically, yet I found ways to offer assistance. I considered the worst-case scenario—extreme flooding with surges up to fifteen feet along the coastlines—and thought of ways to help my son and his family. The area, completely surrounded by water, was not large, but I remained hopeful. I suggested that my son acquire life jackets for the family. They resided in a two-story townhome, which gave me some peace of mind, as they were elevated, but I worried about the water rising above their roof. Although they all knew how to swim, I felt it wasn't enough. I insisted he get life jackets for everyone and rope.

We completed the checklist of additional items needed: sandbags for both the front and back doors, flashlights, cleaning the tubs with bleach and filling them with clean water. The list continued over the following days until all the stores closed in anticipation of the storm. After all, the employees also needed time to prepare for the storm.

Now, at three p.m., both the internet and cable had gone out. The wireless phone service was limited to texts, which seemed to get through, and phone calls, but there was no information from the outside world unless I called a relative or they updated me on the situation. Typically, this area never experienced power outages or cable issues, even with the storm still a few days away.

I called my aunt and my mother to get the latest updates, and my aunt told me that it seemed it would hit south of the Tampa Bay area. It was both a relief and a nightmare; that area would be devastated. It was unimaginable for the region by the water to withstand a twelve to fifteen-foot surge—impossible! Those who didn't evacuate wouldn't be with us anymore. It was the harsh reality of what was ahead.

I strove not to let anxiety overwhelm me. I strove not to become frustrated. I strove to remain calm, knowing this was out of my hands—it was out of everyone's hands. The only one who could manage this storm was God. I had to let go and trust in God. In this situation, there were no winners. We have to accept it as God's will.

It is, "Not My Fight." Even when you're *on the ropes* sometimes, the *referee* calls the fight and declares it as officially, over!

Clinch

Interesting how even in the heat of battle, there's a need for a brief respite to gather strength and refocus. Kind of like life, isn't it? Sometimes, we need to *clinch*, to take a step back, catch our breath, and prepare for the next round. I needed to break free from the grip of emotional exhaustion—to catch my breath, and I seized the moment.

As I drove my SUV up the winding, serpentine driveway, I felt a wave of guilt passing by the valet-parked vehicles, each worth several hundred thousand dollars. The lingering image of a fourteen-year-old boy clinging to a fence in the floodwaters, desperately seeking rescue, stayed in my mind. The countless scenes of people amid absolute ruin were unforgettable. Yet, for just one day, I sought this escape to erase those images and discover a piece of paradise.

Allowing myself this moment of respite was essential, even though the weight of the world still pressed heavily on my heart.

After parking, I stepped out and took in the sight of the perfectly manicured, lush, green landscaping. Being my first time at this location, I felt uncertain about where to enter, so I paused to ask the parking attendants for directions.

Wandering through the lavish halls of this five-star hotel, I was thankful for the break from my extended solitude. It had been days since the sun had kissed my skin or the breeze had brushed against me. Choosing a day pass here was the perfect getaway. The hotel, connected to another equally majestic one, boasted endless corridors. I enjoyed the walk, favoring the stroll's comfort over the ease of valet service. The interior, a shift from my usual taste for modern, showcased a timeless elegance typical of this establishment. Today, I took pleasure in it, pausing to appreciate the intricate window patterns and the art on the walls. The carpets were works of art in themselves. The chandeliers were mesmerizing, and the colors of the walls were classic.

As I approached the hotel lobby doors, the bellman greeted me promptly, and the concierge desk was immediately ready to assist with any needs I had. A nagging discomfort lingered; I wasn't entirely at ease despite the friendliness of the staff.

"Why me, Lord?" I asked. "I found myself pondering, *'Why have I been blessed to be here when so many from my picturesque hometown of Saint Petersburg, FL are displaced?"*

"Have you not endured enough, my child?" I heard God's reassuring voice. *"Did I not vividly show you what your future will look like?"* said God. *"I continue to bestow favor upon you; it is indeed favor,"* God replied. He continued, *"I have searched your heart."*

I began to recite, "*In my father's house are many mansions: if it were not so, I would have told you. I go to prepare a place for you, I will come again, and receive you unto myself; that where I am, there ye may be also.*" John 14:2 (KJV)

Suddenly, another scripture came to my spirit, "*Lay not up for yourselves treasures upon earth, where moth and rust doth corrupt, and *where thieves break through and steal: But lay up for yourselves treasures in heaven, where neither moth nor rust doth corrupt, and where thieves do not break through nor steal: For where your treasure is, there will your heart be also.*" Matthew 6:19-21 (KJV)

In that moment, a smile spread across my face as I was enveloped by a sense of divine tranquility. '*God has prepared a place for me. My treasures are not bound to earthly possessions. God desires for me to enjoy the luxuries, for He considers me worthy of such delights, pleased with the purity He observes in my heart.*

The guilt had dissipated, allowing me to fully embrace what God intended. I found a tranquil corner and began to journal the moments leading up to the big storm.

Hurricane Milton was unyielding, wreaking havoc on Florida's west coast, as the state was already struggling with the consequences of Hurricane Helene's flooding only weeks prior. Houses bobbed on the water as if they were houseboats, and families perched on their rooftops, awaiting rescue by sheriff's boats. Although not as catastrophic as Hurricane Katrina in Louisiana, the conditions in Florida were still dire.

Florida officials had alerted residents to the dangers of wildlife, such as snakes, reptiles, and stingrays, and bacteria that can lead to deadly infections. Shortages of electricity and gasoline affected generators and vehicles alike. With the city's water supply disrupted, widespread chaos ensued.

Fights broke out across gas stations through the Tampa Bay area. Frustration, panic, and fear engulfed those who waited in lines for hours for gas. Cars filled with families. People lined up in a unified line without vehicles. It was something this area had never experienced ever! The periods before, during, and after Milton were akin to a nightmare from the most terrifying horror film.

Milton was brutal—truly brutal. Despite not being new to hurricanes, I realized that one could never outsmart Mother Nature. Many undeserving people suffered; it was heart-wrenching to witness the extensive devastation and loss throughout Florida. The loss of life and the devastation of staple restaurants and hotel businesses across various coastal communities was profound. Waterfront properties, both luxurious homes and those of hardworking individuals from upper, middle, and impoverished classes suffered equally. The flooding was so severe that cars were submerged in murky waters, and roofs were torn from stadiums and amphitheaters.

Yet, amidst all the suffering, people discovered *hope, community, purpose*, and *a new direction*. They reconnected with *family* and *friends*. The crisis tested and gauged individuals' faith; some lost theirs, while others found it stronger than ever. Emotions ran the gamut from inconsolable tears to anger. Observing from a distance due to a mandatory evacuation, it was utterly astonishing.

I had grappled with a mix of emotions that I couldn't quite identify, but I knew there was more troubling me than just the sadness from the destruction. I came across a social media post from a meteorologist stating: "*Hurricane fatigue* is real. After a major hurricane event, many people, no longer fueled by adrenaline, will experience a crash—both physically and emotionally. This often doesn't occur immediately but can happen weeks or even months later. It's normal to feel this way, and you're not alone." Hurricane fatigue is a real and acknowledged condition.

That was the moment of realization; *what I was going through was not unique—many others I had spoken to were experiencing the same at different times. This was normal. We weren't losing our sanity. We would persevere!*

Like many others, I had been away from home for nearly a week, unsure of what awaited me upon return. The power outage had cut off my camera monitoring system, leaving me in the dark about any potential damage—a concern I shared with countless others in different places. The journey back was chaotic, with some taking to the skies and others hitting the road. Airports were swamped, and highways were jammed with miles of traffic, all of us eager to get back to our homes.

Every year, I allocated money for the hurricane season to cover expected costs like potential hotel stays, fuel, and cash withdrawals—it's just a part of life in sunny Florida. Yet this year had proven to be especially costly. My funds dwindled rapidly! The storms had been non-stop, hitting back-to-back. Currently, we were monitoring a third potential storm forming in the tropics. "It's quite unusual for a system to develop this far out in the Atlantic in mid-October."

Seated in the hotel's bar lounge, I pondered the number of fellow evacuees from Tampa Bay and those from different states. The place was bustling with men in jerseys, families, and groups of colleagues. Taking a deep breath, I contemplated the situation. *Every event teaches us something; it's all part of a greater plan for growth. I am determined to discover the "lesson" and "purpose" that this experience is meant to teach me.*

Some might argue, "Oh, it's just life. Life happens to the best of us." And while I won't disagree that it's all part of life, I still believe that if we don't view the situations that greatly impact us as tools to build resilience, then we won't be better equipped to handle them when they recur, not just for ourselves but to assist others as well.

Indeed, there are many lessons to be learned. Paramount among these is the art of maintaining one's peace amidst chaos. Only days ago, I had been consumed with anxiety because my son and three beloved grandchildren refused to evacuate in advance of the hurricane, leaving me terrified for their safety. Now, here I was, surrounded by such tranquility and beauty.

It's astonishing how quickly things can change.

I will always remember my son telling me, "*If it's my time, Mom, then it's my time.*" But it wasn't just about him; it was about the welfare of my grandchildren too.

My eldest grandson is a true blessing; his gorgeous brown eyes are the windows to his soul, reflecting his remarkable devotion to God, family, and humanity, which is truly commendable. His athletic leadership and academic achievements are admirable. Each grandchild excels academically and possesses unique talents. My granddaughter at birth was the epitome of beauty, flawless in every way, resembling a delicate porcelain doll. Her talents mirror my own childhood passions—writing, drawing, music, and embracing her femininity. The youngest grandchild exudes confidence, charming and exasperating in equal measure, always leaving a grand impression. All of them are beautiful children, endearing themselves to everyone they meet.

Hence, you can comprehend why I wished to spare them from such a distressing experience. It was simply too much to bear.

I questioned myself, *does my son possess greater faith than I do?* After all, he had endured experiences beyond my comprehension. His faith had been put to the test time and again. As his parents, his father and I, have nurtured him in the teachings of God. "*Train up a child in the way he should go, and when he is old, he will not depart from it.*" Proverbs 22:6 (KJV).

In our absence, we gave our son the greatest protection a parent can offer—faith in and reliance upon God alone.

As the power outage lingered, it tested our endurance, leaving us without our usual comforts and battling the heat. But then, like knights in shining armor, linemen from afar came to our rescue, bringing back the light. We waited, thankful, knowing they came to aid, not to be faulted. Still, some simmered with impatience, craving swift solutions, unaware of nature's calming embrace. Porches turned into sanctuaries, strolls offered relief, and kids found delight in outdoor games, breaking away from the hold of digital devices.

Everyone's suffering is unique, as is the duration and the story behind it. During the hurricane, I briefly reflected on who reached out to me and who didn't, who I felt compelled to check on, and who I inadvertently forgot. The right relationships are crucial in these times. God will reveal them to you. It's your responsibility to nurture these relationships so they can thrive. Welcome those who genuinely support your growth into the person God intended you to be. They don't arrive to disturb your peace like a nocturnal hurricane; they come as "sunshine after the storm." *Consider who brings turmoil and who brings light.*

Indeed, life needs both sunshine and rain for growth, but each in its own time. Overwatering a seed will stifle its growth, not nurture it. Let yourself grow incrementally, fostered by the right connections. Examine how you form relationships and your role within them. Do you bring tranquility and enrich others' lives, or are you a burden they can't bear?

I would rather step back than disrupt someone's peace. Inner peace radiates outward to others.

As I commuted hours in traffic back to Tampa Bay, it felt foreign. Driving in traffic again a normalcy. But everything was not normal. As I rode along the highway, I could see the devastation; huge light poles stricken to the ground. The amphitheater near the casino had taken quite the beating and lost! Highway signs and debris were displaced equally; it was safe to say everyone had to drive with a great measure of caution. Although there were clear signs a storm had been through the area, I had not quite neared my home. I had to cross a bay of water to get to my residence, and, boy, I was not prepared.

As I neared, I thought *Hmmm, not much damage. This is good.*

Yet the closer I came to my destination, the more I could see of the destruction. Enormous trees aligned in a perfect row along the bridge were uprooted from the water, their roots massive. I had never seen anything like this from any other storm.

What in the world? I looked on, astonished. I could not believe what my eyes were revealing to me.

As I entered my community, there was no visible damage to the beautiful palm trees welcoming me to my residence. The garage was still intact, with no visible standing water. Everything appeared intact, unlike the storm of hurricane Helene, where things had been tossed and destroyed only weeks prior.

As I proceeded from the garage, indoors… I was not prepared for the stench that hit my nostrils; it smelled of dirty baby diapers, but there were no babies! It was coming from my kitchen refrigerator and freezer. I immediately placed everything that I had in my hands down and opened the windows. Then, I proceeded to turn on my home fragrance diffuser tower. I had to begin to clear out the refrigerator of the spoiled food. Every condiment, every drink, every food item, everything in the freezer had to be tossed out. After discarding everything, I got bleach and water and attempted to remove the smell. After cleaning it at least three times, the smell still was not removed. I had to turn to other measures and begin my search for baking soda.

I was tired from the long drive and traffic, to then having to clear out my refrigerator. My body was aching, and I was mentally drained. I felt overwhelmed. I took a warm shower and hit the bed. Extreme exhaustion and pain overcoming me.

I've never felt like this before or after a hurricane, what is happening? I wondered.

As I lay in bed, my mind began to drift…

How could this be happening? Just weeks ago, I was in Miami for a late birthday celebration, living my best life in the finest of hotels south Florida could offer—and now, here I am, air filled with stench after being evacuated for a week and my body feeling aches like never before! What has really happened here amidst Florida?! Two major hurricanes within weeks of one another affecting the bay area; this is absolutely unimaginable.

I tried hard not to let anxiety fill my chest, striving to keep feelings of aggravation at bay as I realized that this storm hit me so hard because I'd endured a lot of loss this year. The death of my beloved grandmother, a dear male friend, and the finalization of my marriage—divorce. The weight of so much loss in one year was overwhelming. It felt like a category 5 hurricane had struck my life, and it was a lot to bear.

Nevertheless, it was my duty to take the necessary steps to restore peace and achieve a healthy mental balance. I started counseling to better manage my emotions, as I have never been a proponent of using stimulants to regulate moods. While I'm not opposed to their use for those with a chemical imbalance, my need was for someone to listen without judgment and provide strategies to help me return to my path.

For me, it was "*the art of preserving peace...*" within my own realm.

Bob and Weave

The mental weight took me back to a familiar place I had been before… I felt myself crashing, bobbing and weaving, dodging the blows, and trying to stay composed amidst the chaos. Which was why it was so important for me to get counseling when I felt overcome with emotions during the hurricanes. It felt like something I had experienced before was brewing, and I knew exactly what it could possibly lead up to…

Recognizing the signs early on and seeking help through counseling was a crucial step in protecting my mental health. The hurricanes, both literal and metaphorical, stirred up a storm within me that needed addressing to avoid falling into a deeper struggle… *Another T.K.O. that once had me seeing stars.*

It had been my breaking point years prior. For the first time ever, I had experienced a meltdown of epic proportions. I had been clueless about what was happening, but I had zero cares about the audience. I unleashed all my fury, and of all days, it had happened on Christmas day years ago.

The astonishment on everyone's faces was unmistakable; my ordeal was incomprehensible to them. It represented the culmination of years of trauma. The emotional abuse I endured seemed to stem from generational patterns, unintentionally perpetuated by those unaware of their actions. In seeking a better future, I aimed to ensure that my son would learn from my experiences and my grandchildren would witness a more positive example. Breaking the cycle had to start with **me**!

Reflecting on that moment, it's clear how much I had been holding in... until I couldn't anymore. The pressure, the emotions, everything erupted in a way I had never experienced before. It was a pivotal moment, a wake-up call that something needed to change.

The significance of it happening on Christmas day only added to the intensity of the memory. A day typically filled with joy and celebration turned into a personal battle. It was a stark reminder of the importance of addressing our inner struggles and not letting them fester until they explode.

Call me *done, overcooked, ready to be served*. After years of biting my tongue, playing the turn-the-other-cheek game, and pardoning the endless parade of disrespect and double standards, I'd had enough! I checked out of that emotional circus right then and there. I finally **let go**.

It felt like a massive weight had been lifted off my shoulders. I realized that my peace and mental health were far more important than maintaining relationships that brought me nothing but pain and frustration, even if it came from *people I loved*. It wasn't an easy decision, but it was necessary for my own well-being. By cutting ties, I made room for healing and growth.

In the days, weeks, and months following my meltdown, I found solace in quiet solitude, tending to my wounds and hesitating to share my struggles with many. *Why?* Because some people find pleasure in another's misfortune, especially in times of vulnerability. I refused to give them that satisfaction. My faith was unwavering, believing that God would guide me out of the shadows. It was a place of desolation, where I felt wronged by those I had only meant to love.

During this time, I held onto my faith, trusting that God would lead me toward healing and strength. It was a journey of introspection and resilience, finding comfort in the belief that brighter days were ahead. Despite the hurt and isolation, I learned to rely on my inner strength and the divine guidance that assured me I was never truly alone.

Those moments of isolation, though challenging, can also be times of profound reflection and growth. Shielding myself from the judgment and ill intentions of others was necessary for my self-preservation. My faith and resilience carried me through the darkest times, illuminating a path toward healing and understanding.

On that Christmas, I made a resolute decision to remove myself from the dysfunction permanently. It was the last time I allowed myself to be overwhelmed by those feelings. I vowed never to let those individuals push me to that state again. To this day, I have upheld that vow, and it has been years since I made that promise.

The journey of healing and self-discovery has indeed been challenging but immensely rewarding. Each step forward has reinforced my commitment to creating a healthier environment for myself and those I love. Setting extreme boundaries was a decision not made lightly but was necessary for my emotional well-being.

How did I reach that point? I yearned for so much more from life. There was no way this was going to be the entirety of my story. I realized I had much more to offer the world, but I also knew that until I lived authentically, as God intended for me, I couldn't help anyone else.

My desire to witness to others and help them find their path was overshadowed by my past choices, leaving no space for future endeavors. Despite this, God persistently guided me toward self-healing. The Holy Spirit encouraged me, showing me that not everything had to be a struggle and that I could approach things differently.

God gradually taught me to communicate more effectively: to listen with the intent to understand, not defend—a principle we've all been told, but it holds profound truth. When you truly listen to understand, compassion for others can flourish. This shift in perspective opened up new pathways for growth and fulfillment.

As I embraced authenticity and heeded divine guidance, I began to see the potential for a better future. I started to understand that my past did not define me but rather shaped me into who I am today. My experiences became a source of strength, empowering me to help others more effectively.

Living authentically allowed me to reconnect with my true self and align my actions with my beliefs. This alignment brought a sense of peace and purpose that I had longed for. It became clear that the journey of self-discovery and healing was not just for my own benefit but also to serve as a testament to the transformative power of faith and resilience.

Jab

You know, some might say I lacked discernment because of all I've been through. It's almost like they throw that *jab* at me because I was so trusting during my thirties and forties. But here's the thing—God knows our hearts. He understands who truly benefits us. Every bit of pain I went through had a purpose. Every relationship, every *high* and *low*—it all happened for a reason, and it's shaped me into who I am today.

When I look back, I realize that trusting others, despite the risks, was part of my journey. Those experiences brought unforgettable highs and taught me invaluable lessons. God used every moment to guide me and help me understand my purpose better. It's these moments that have prepared me for what lies ahead.

Nonetheless, I firmly believe in *forgiveness*. I believe people can find their way back and change, but only if there is genuine repentance and transformation. I will not permit someone to reenter my life without these conditions being met. The choice is mine to make, not theirs. If I sense no real change, I will not deceive myself into thinking otherwise.

My journey has taught me the importance of discerning who truly deserves a place in my life. While forgiveness is essential for my own peace, it does not mean allowing toxic patterns to persist. True change requires sincere effort and a willingness to grow. Without this, it's impossible to rebuild trust.

I have learned to protect my heart and ensure that only those who respect my boundaries are welcomed back.

Wisdom guides us to a place of peace because our experiences prepare us for the future. The choice we face is whether to repeat our past misfortunes or to make wiser decisions that propel us to new heights in this world.

Feeling loved, supported, and understood is crucial. We need to rest in places where we are spiritually and emotionally nourished. It's vital to recognize environments that align with our purpose. Letting go of people and habits that once brought comfort can be challenging, but reaching a point where there's no return to those harmful influences is essential for growth.

Sometimes, we search for peace that's always been within us, yet we give it away too easily to those who don't appreciate our worth. Or perhaps they do recognize it, which is why they walk away or choose not to move forward. These individuals often come in and out of our lives, searching for something they've had but didn't recognize.

I had to come to terms with the idea that every person we meet may only be there for *seasonal* purposes. Time reveals their role.

Life's storms kick up painful experiences that can knock the wind out of us when we least expect it. We're all fallible, part of the human race, each carrying our own burdens and sins. But it's up to us—only us—to decide what's beneficial for our lives. *What do we desire? What are our boundaries? What truly makes us happy and fulfills our purpose? What relationships are healthy for our well-being?*

I have come to understand that the decisions I face are solely mine to make, without the need for debate. The freedom of choice is uniquely my own. This realization has led me to appreciate the tranquility I possess, establish solid boundaries, and cultivate relationships that provide encouragement and support. My experiences have illuminated the importance of leading a life that is in harmony with my genuine purpose.

Throughout my life, I have made choices that were not ideal. I have inflicted pain upon myself, permitted others to cause me pain, and have been the source of pain for others. However, there comes a time when we must cease to perpetuate hurt and begin the process of healing. Recognizing that even the best among us can falter is essential, learning from our past mistakes with the hope of not repeating them.

The individuals we welcome into our lives reflect our judgment of character. If they turn out to be detrimental, it challenges our own discernment in allowing them into our thoughts, lives, and personal spaces. Everything starts with us. We have the freedom to make choices. *Will you choose tranquility?* We control the temperament of our relationships. If they prove toxic, *why keep them around?* Continuing to engage with them only delays your own peace.

When we hit a crossroad, we have the power to choose peace and shape our own path. Own that power. There will be times when life's relentless blows will hit you hard, but remember, it's in these tough moments that our true strength and resilience shine through. Hold on to that power and keep moving forward, even when things seem overwhelming.

Allow people with issues the space to work on themselves. You are not their savior and you do not have the power to save anyone—recognize this as truth! Repeat after me: It's 'Not My Fight!'

Understanding this truth is essential. You can offer support and compassion, but, ultimately, everyone must take responsibility for their own healing and growth. Your own peace and well-being should always be a priority.

Embrace this mantra, and focus on nurturing yourself and your own journey.

Cross

Friendships can be a complex and sometimes painful journey, especially when betrayal is involved. It's heartbreaking to think about how my trust was shattered not once but twice by those I considered *friends*. The pain of discovering such betrayals, especially after offering my home and support, is unimaginable.

I had two female friends who were both intimate with men I had been involved with. One betrayal I didn't find out about until years later. I had invited her to live in my home and later found out through a man she was seeing that it had happened. I had always suspected but never had real proof. *I still don't.*

She was dating the best friend of the man I was seeing, who lived in another state but visited frequently. So, when she said she was at his house, it didn't seem strange at the time.

Years later, through someone she was seeing and broke up with, I *finally* learned the truth! He wrote to me, sharing that she was *not a true friend, was jealous of me, spoke harshly about me, and had slept with the person I was involved with.* Shame on both of them, but especially on her! I haven't spoken to either of them in years. I doubt they know that I actually know—neither were worth confronting. I pray that they both are better people now; one can only hope.

Some might say that maybe the person who told me was trying to get back at her for some reason or wanted to talk to me. I don't recall him making an advance toward me. I knew it was true; I felt it in my *gut* everything that this man said to me was true. It's sad because I was there for this woman when no one else was—not her family, not any man she was involved with. She was sleeping in her luxury car with no place to stay, and I gave her a roof over her head. In my own home, I would wake to hear her talking about me to someone on the other end of the line. She knew her time was limited. She had no respect for my home.

There's a difference between being *nice* and being a *fool*. I was no longer going to be a fool for this woman. I had been too good of a friend in more ways than I can explain. No one knows why women move the way they do—often, it's because of betrayal and hurt from another woman, just as they've experienced hurt from a man.

Crossing others is something many people do because of a lack of self-worth and integrity. They often repeat the hurtful actions that were once done to them. Betrayal and jealousy are experiences I have faced many times in my lifetime. This is why I rarely click instantly with other women; I prefer to sit back, observe their behavior, and watch how they move. Although others may not have done exactly what those individuals did to me, my experiences have taught me to proceed with caution. And if we've had multiple encounters where trust has been broken, my self-protection mechanism will kick in. I won't keep them around; instead, I'll love them from a distance and wish them all of life's blessings.

Experience guides us with wisdom, and we must learn to use it and apply it where necessary. It's essential to recognize the patterns in others' behavior and protect ourselves from potential harm. By being discerning, we can foster healthier relationships and avoid repeating past mistakes.

My experiences have shaped my perspective on friendships and trust. While I remain open to new connections, I now prioritize observing and understanding the true intentions of others. This strategy allows me to build relationships based on mutual respect and trust, rather than rushing into connections that may not be genuine.

Blocking

You dedicate yourself to those who ignore you, dishonor your emotions, and will never value you! People can only exploit you if you permit it. Is one compelled to remain out of love? At what point must one depart to maintain their sanity or peace of mind?

I have found relationships challenging, leading me to face difficult questions.

Why were they unsuccessful?

What part did I play in their failure, even though I faced disrespect?

Is there anything I could have done differently?

I departed because I realized it was **"Not My Fight."** At the time, I lacked the necessary life experiences to address the issues that had taken root long before our paths crossed. The unresolved conflicts and buried emotions were like invisible chains holding me back from truly understanding myself and the complexities of our relationship.

Indeed, I had my own baggage. Yet not all items fit into the same suitcase. Some are for carry-on, others for check-in, and some just for the purse. Suffice it to say, I've handled some real carry-on baggage—far too bulky for a standard flight. As I journeyed on, I realized that the direction in which my intended destination was heading didn't appeal to me. The paths those journeys were leading to no longer aligned with what I wanted.

After enduring many years in various situations, I realized I had to save myself. *How many have departed knowing that staying would not end well? How often do we lack the will to act in our best interest?*

The adage goes, "*Some people bring out the best in you, while others bring out the worst.*" It's essential to draw closer to those who enhance our lives and pull away from those who have not self-improved. I came across a social media post stating, "*Some are single because they're too smart!*" I laughed, grasping the meaning. Often in relationships, I wasn't seeking the truth, but still, the pieces failed to align.

I've discovered a truth about myself, which I believe holds true for many: once respect for someone is lost, the relationship is effectively over. Words then cut deeper than anything salvageable. Actions become hurtful, care diminishes, and the heart bleeds openly.

I'm the type who at times can wear my heart on my sleeve, and if I seek honesty but someone chooses otherwise, then respect is lost. My personality is straightforward: what you see is what you get. *My smile is real.* If we don't mesh, I won't pretend—we might stay cordial, but there's no spark, platonic or romantic. I've ended friendships when trust was shattered and vibes felt wrong. As an *empath*, you can't mask your true energy from me; it reveals itself every time.

I became cautious about who I let into my life, particularly after my divorce. Being close to me was indeed a privilege; it meant there was something unique about you. I could bond with sincere hearts, not necessarily perfect people, because nobody is perfect, myself included. Yet some connections, though imperfect, fit seamlessly into your life. These connections are the ones that maintain *peace* in your life; they are meant to *enrich*, not to spoil.

There are also people worth rebuilding trust with when those individuals are painfully putting in the work to not cause the same pain once inflicted—not because they want to be a part of your life but because they recognize the need for change.

One may discern that a person is at war with themselves if they are perpetually in conflict with others, whether at home, work, or elsewhere, unable to find peace. Peace, indeed, lies within. Many struggle internally because they have not yet healed from past traumas, such as childhood experiences, relationship breakdowns, or unfulfilled dreams.

It's important to realize that there's little you can do for someone who is struggling with their own internal conflicts; these are battles that began long before you entered the picture.

Whether it's a man or woman dealing with the shadows of abandonment, the wounds of past relationships, or the struggle against substance abuse, it's important to remember that these issues didn't start yesterday. You don't have to be the hero in their story. They need to reach that pivotal moment where they crave change more than a late-night snack and declare, 'Enough is enough!' They must get to a point where they are tired of the same old patterns in relationships and jobs, and make a solid decision to say, 'No more repeats of the same old story!'

It's about them finding the strength within themselves to break free from those cycles and embrace a new path.

Why are you fighting with your ex, your children's mother/father? You know how they operate. Stop allowing them to consume you. Stop giving them power over your life. Move differently. Be mindful. Be intentional. Be swift to escape fights that are within that individual. The fight is within themselves.

Remind yourself, "Not My Fight" The Art of Preserving Peace.

Knockout

In life, there will be battles that are meant for you, as well as those that are beyond your capacity. You may be too strong or not strong enough. Regardless, engage in the battles that align with your purpose and current stage in life.

Had I engaged only in battles that were truly mine, numerous situations might have concluded differently. I acknowledge this. We must take responsibility for our choices and decisions, facing the consequences maturely without casting blame on others when we are involved.

An ex-partner once labeled me as *damaged,* and he took partial responsibility for his part in the damage he claims he caused. I rebuked that label. His words *did not define me.* I did not accept his words as truth! To him, I might have seemed damaged, but I used his words as a catalyst for self-improvement, addressing the flaws he perceived in me. I firmly believe that people reveal their true selves, and I never doubt God's power. If God allows us to see another day, it means we have a purpose to accomplish.

Indeed, I am perpetually evolving—absolutely. Yet no one holds the power to define **WHO I AM**. I possess full awareness of my identity and the values I uphold, and I am not 'damaged goods.' The notion is absurd. I am not the same person I was yesterday. *Trust me, you will not find me where you left me.*

In that brief period, he had to retract his words... whether he realized it or not. I put in the effort, sought counseling to gain insights I might have lacked. Truthfully, even the counselor seemed impressed. She remarked that I radiated an inner brightness and possessed the potential to impact many lives.

Never let anyone label you, especially not as 'damaged.' *You are healed.*

Those previous knockdown, drawn-out fights were never my fights... dealing with people who had issues of their own that had nothing to do with me yet infringed their insecurities onto me because I am someone who knows what I bring to any table that I am invited to. And if I'm not invited, I'm okay with that; I will create a table where I can sit at the head.

Don't ever stop praying for others' deliverance—it will make the world a better place. Allow them to gossip. Let them speak ill. Let them utter unkind words behind your back. For no person of success wastes their time disparaging others who strive to improve their lives. You will keep improving. They will persist in their negativity. In the end, it's clear who is truly succeeding. Concentrate on the lessons learned, rather than the pain that suffering brings.

The lives you are destined to touch, you shall. Trust in God to ensure it. Let God lead the way. Cease the struggle, relinquish control. Welcome God to navigate your path. Permit His hand to dictate the pace, to hasten or to halt. And when He chooses to slow you down, understand it's to avoid a potential hazard. In divine timing, all will be revealed: the reasons for delays, the unsuitability of a partner, the silence after a job interview, the collapse of a deal. God has grander plans. *Can you wait with patience for His timing?*

Realizing that you can't please everyone is the first step to a more serene life. So, take a breath and stop trying to. And stop trying to figure out 'every next step…'

This year, the game-changer for me was the power of spoken words—*affirmations*. The instant I started vocalizing my desires and my convictions about what I would have in my life, everything began to align in my favor. Not by deeds alone, but it became accessible to me! **Accessible to me**! *Can you hear me?*

Only God, who sits above, can see everything. We cannot know everything; we must walk our own paths with pride. What God has in store for you is yours alone—believe in it, have faith in it, trust it, and walk in it.

Foul

Despite the world's ever-present judgment, my profound connection with God remained steadfast. The Holy Spirit never let me down. I could always sense its guidance, especially when encountering someone whose spirit was off. With my gift of empathy, I felt emotions deeply, and my spirit would alert me to those who would later prove less loyal than they seemed. This unease would become unsettling in my spirit until the truth was revealed.

As I lay in bed, contemplating my past experiences, I was keenly aware that God had always been by my side. However, this time felt different; hope seemed just out of reach. Although I believed this wasn't the end of my story, the way forward was unclear, and this new life felt foreign to me.

As a newlywed, I found myself in a sprawling, beautiful house within a prestigious, gated, golf course community. We owned luxurious exotic cars. On the surface, my husband and I made an impressive couple. He was a retired military man who had successfully transitioned to a civilian career. By all appearances, our life should have been perfect.

Navigating this divide was incredibly tough. The disparity between how things appeared and how they truly were created an emotional turbulence that was hard to manage. The pressure to maintain a facade while internally grappling with so much turmoil was exhausting.

In those moments, it felt like a lonely journey, as the external world seemed oblivious to the true challenges I faced.

This disparity left me questioning everything—my decisions, my expectations, and even my faith. The material success and societal status couldn't mask the emotional turmoil and disconnect I felt. It was a reminder that true fulfillment and peace don't come from external trappings but from within. As I navigated this new chapter, I realized that the journey ahead would require not just external adjustments but a deep, introspective transformation as well.

I had never dated anyone like my husband. He had distinct European features—extremely handsome with a lighter complexion, and his hair was a fascinating mix of curls and straight strands. He stood out, the very man my friends had always pictured for me. His presence was captivating, and he embodied a charm that was both intriguing and endearing.

Reflecting on the early days of our relationship, it's clear how much his unique attributes fascinated me. Despite the initial allure, I soon realized that the journey of a relationship goes far beyond external appearances. The real challenge was reconciling the outer persona with the inner realities, both for myself and for him.

After a year of dating and a year of being engaged, we tied the knot in a beautiful gondola ceremony. That's where the fairytale both began and ended. Incredibly, we argued on our wedding day. As I approached the gondolas, I didn't see my soon-to-be husband anywhere in sight. I found a quiet area in a corner and paced, asking myself, *"Are you sure?" "Should you really be doing this?"* The groom was late; later I was told that both the soles of his shoes had ripped apart. How does this happen on one's wedding day? Surely, it should have been a sign from God that we both were not ready… yet we proceeded with the ceremony.

From the outside, it seemed too perfect for such a thing to happen, but it did. As the bride who had waited years to remarry, I was deeply invested in the moment. Despite this, we exchanged vows. I clung to every word from the officiant, while my soon-to-be husband was more focused on smiling for the strangers behind the cameras.

It was clear that the fairytale facade masked underlying issues that couldn't be ignored. The cracks that appeared, even on such a significant day, were signals that all was not as perfect as it seemed. It was a lesson in the importance of addressing the real issues beneath the surface, rather than being swept away by the outward beauty of the occasion.

It's amazing how God can grant the desires of your heart, even when you're not ready to embrace them. That was our story—we were completely unprepared for the attention, the lifestyle, and the marriage. We were at vastly different stages in our lives. I had a significant gap between my first marriage and my second, giving me time to reflect and grow alone, while my husband hadn't experienced the same solitude.

Looking back, I have no doubt that he loved me, but it wasn't the forever love that I was ready for. His actions were driven more by the fear of losing me rather than a true readiness for lifelong commitment. This misalignment became clearer as time went on, revealing that our emotional readiness for such a significant step was different. The disparity in our life experiences and emotional maturity meant that while I was prepared for the depth and endurance of a lifelong partnership, he wasn't. This realization, though painful, was vital in understanding the dynamics of our relationship and the foundation on which it was built.

Navigating these realizations was a transformative experience. It required honesty and introspection to see the truth of our situation. While the process was challenging, it ultimately led to a deeper understanding of what I truly needed and deserved in a relationship.

In the end, he was a great provider. I can never say he wasn't there for our household or for me financially. He ensured we had everything we needed materially, and I will always be grateful for that. But emotionally, neither of us were ready for the baggage that surfaced in our marriage. We were completely unprepared for the complex emotional dynamics that a committed relationship entails. A beautiful home wasn't enough to sustain us.

We both found ourselves increasingly miserable, though I felt the weight of it more deeply. In his reality, he continued living the lifestyle of a single man—not by staying out all night but by being emotionally absent even when he was physically present. It was killing me softly. I was losing myself because I had never experienced a man showing so little interest in me. It was a stark contrast to the man who had gone to great lengths to court me, the man who had once made me feel cherished and valued.

Reflecting on those times, it's evident that our emotional disconnect overshadowed the material comfort we enjoyed. His absence, even when he was there, left a void that I couldn't ignore. The disparity between his financial support and his emotional presence highlighted a critical gap in our relationship.

The reality of our situation was incredibly challenging. It became clear that a fulfilling relationship requires more than just material provisions; it demands genuine emotional connection and mutual engagement. The lack of these elements gradually eroded the foundation of our marriage, leading to a profound sense of isolation and unhappiness.

Blending families is a tough gig, and ours was no exception. We came from completely different backgrounds, and out of respect for everyone involved, I'll just say it wasn't easy. But, hey, I learned some important pearls of wisdom along the way. First, keep family out of your relationship drama. Seriously. You might forgive and move on, but your family and friends will hold onto those grudges forever. It's best to keep them out of it unless they're professionals who can actually help.

Another nugget I picked up is the importance of clear, honest communication. Misunderstandings can spiral out of control when you're trying to merge different lifestyles, traditions, and expectations. Being open and straightforward about feelings, needs, and boundaries can save a lot of heartache.

Patience is another key element. Blending families doesn't happen overnight. It takes time for everyone to adjust and find their place in the new family dynamic. Understanding and accepting that this process is gradual can help reduce frustration and unrealistic expectations.

Lastly, never underestimate the power of empathy. Everyone involved is going through a transition, and showing compassion and understanding toward each other's experiences can build a stronger, more unified family unit.

At our age, you'd think we would have known better, and in many ways, we did. But trust me, our issues were so severe that neither of us knew how to handle the other. Our communication styles were worlds apart. He was from up north, and I was from the south, so there were significant cultural differences in our values. What he felt was justified, I saw as extremely disrespectful. It was a constant clash of perspectives that we couldn't seem to reconcile.

Being a writer, I naturally found writing to be a much more effective form of communication for me than speaking. I tried to convey my thoughts and feelings through letters and notes more times than I can count, but often to no avail—at least, not immediately. It was frustrating, feeling like my words were falling on deaf ears. Writing allowed me to express myself clearly and thoughtfully, but it didn't always bridge the gap in our communication struggles.

Reflecting on these challenges, it's clear how important understanding and compromise are in a relationship. The cultural and communication differences created a barrier that was difficult to overcome. Writing was my way of reaching out, of trying to connect and express my emotions, but it wasn't always enough to make him understand.

This experience highlighted the necessity of finding common ground in communication styles and cultural values. It taught me that while writing can be a powerful tool, it also requires the other person to be receptive and open to understanding. True connection involves both parties making an effort to bridge the gaps and learn from each other's perspectives.

Next, don't judge people based on their looks, lifestyle, or family background. It's crucial to be open-minded about how much you can learn and grow from differences. If more people saw the value in diversity, blending families wouldn't be so scary for newcomers. Despite the extremely bitter nature of our divorce, my ex-husband (my son's father) and I always made it a point to introduce any serious partners to each other. We felt it was crucial to know who our child would be around. This was a non-negotiable rule with no exceptions. Ensuring our child's safety and stability was a priority, even amidst the changes in our personal lives.

And lastly, respect is key for everyone involved. A blended family can only thrive if there's mutual respect and understanding. It's not about how perfect everything looks on the outside—what matters is the emotional connection and respect within the family.

My then-husband and his exes—what a roller coaster and nightmare all at the same time. However, now that I have discovered true peace, I realize that I brought this upon myself. If I hadn't sought answers, if I hadn't approached those who never made a vow to me, I could have spared myself much heartache. It was excruciating to accept that the battle was not with those women but with him. I believed those women should have recognized that this man was married, yet they showed no self-respect, seeking only their own satisfaction and clearly had no respect for their own relationships. I pray that God has mercy on the karma that has the potential to ricochet like a boomerang.

Coming to terms with this reality was incredibly painful, but it also marked the beginning of a journey toward true peace and self-awareness. Acknowledging that the real conflict lay within my own relationship and not with those external to it was a difficult but necessary step. It required a profound shift in perspective, allowing me to focus on the core issues and prioritize my own well-being.

This experience deepens the importance of self-respect and the need to set boundaries within relationships. It taught me that seeking answers from those outside the commitment can often lead to more heartache and confusion. True resolution comes from within the relationship through honest communication and mutual understanding.

The journey to peace involved forgiving myself for the mistakes made and learning to trust my instincts and judgment. It highlighted the significance of inner strength and the power of self-reflection. Moving forward, I have a clearer understanding of what I deserve and the kind of relationships that align with my values and well-being.

In truth, I disrespected myself by remaining in that relationship too long, one that was detrimental to my overall well-being. From the start, I knew who I was and what I needed. He simply did not possess what was necessary to give to me. He did not know how. He tried with the tools that he had been using in every relationship prior to me. And I didn't want to feel like a failure. It was my second marriage. I just didn't want to give up on us. I stayed, hoping that the man I saw in the year of courtship would show up for more than a week or two at a time. What I've observed, not just in my ex-husband but in many others, including women, is that people bear scars they don't know how to heal. They mask these wounds with temporary fixes in addictive behaviors, which can lead to a downward spiral. If one is not careful, they too may fall into this pit. You might wonder why these individuals don't take a break to work on themselves. The truth is, confronting past traumas is painful. However, failing to address these issues means carrying the pain from one relationship to another, potentially for a lifetime.

This realization reinforces the importance of self-respect and the courage it takes to acknowledge when a relationship is no longer serving one's well-being. The hope that *things will improve, the fear of failure,* and *the desire to salvage something once promising* can often cloud judgment. But recognizing the necessity of change is the first step toward healing and growth.

Many people, indeed, carry unresolved trauma that manifests in their relationships. Temporary fixes and avoidance only perpetuate a cycle of pain. Confronting these deep-seated issues is daunting, yet it is essential for genuine healing and personal growth. The path to healing involves facing those fears and scars, seeking support, and allowing oneself the space and time to rebuild and transform.

Below the Belt

So, life decided to throw me a curveball...

Just after my ex-husband and I met, I found myself in a massive multi-vehicle accident—it was like something out of a movie. This kicked off a whirlwind of doctor visits, endless physical therapy sessions, and more tests than I could count. Eventually, they sent me in for an MRI, which led to visits with a neurologist.

My neurologist was like a detective, analyzing what the MRI revealed about my brain. Still, neither of us could figure out why I wasn't getting any better. The mystery continued! I was prescribed medication to regulate my mood and manage these killer migraines, which was a new experience for me since I had never touched recreational drugs or brain-affecting prescriptions before.

Then things got even more interesting—I found myself struggling to find the right words or finish sentences. Imagine having your spouse step in like some kind of impromptu speechwriter! It was clear something was seriously off, but my brain decided to keep things mysterious.

Living with these limitations was a daily challenge. The confident, articulate person I once was seemed to be slipping away, replaced by someone who had to fight to express even the simplest thoughts. It was both an emotional and psychological battle as much as a physical one, testing my strength in ways I never imagined.

Despite my husband's support, the journey felt solitary, marked by inner turmoil that I couldn't easily share or explain. The accident had changed my life in profound ways I was still coming to terms with, and the road to recovery was long and uncertain. It required not just physical healing but also an adjustment to a new reality, where each day brought new challenges.

While lying in bed, I started to hallucinate. This had only happened once before, during a childhood bout with chicken pox. Now, I was seeing enormous spiders. In the mirror, my face appeared grotesquely distorted. I found myself pulling at my hair, which seemed all wrong. The reflection gazing back at me was unrecognizable. After several adjustments to my medication in an attempt to acclimate to a mood-altering drug, I felt lost. It was as if I had ceased to exist.

Experiencing such intense hallucinations and feeling disconnected from my own identity was incredibly frightening and isolating. The combination of physical injury, psychological stress, and the side effects of medication created a complex web of challenges that tested my resilience in unimaginable ways.

Often, we collide with the very things we try to escape. Such was my life.

After a prolonged period of unsatisfactory exchanges with my neurologist, both of us became increasingly frustrated and still without a solution. Eventually, I was referred to a neuropsychologist. This expert conducted comprehensive memory tests and held in-depth discussions with my husband and me about everything, from our childhoods to our present lives. Finally, I experienced some relief. I received practical tools and strategies to help me manage the multitude of diagnoses I had been given. I felt overwhelmed yet relieved.

Implementing these strategies daily at home and in my interactions with my husband led to significant improvements in our household functioning. The neuropsychologist recommended that I avoid traditional work environments for two years to aid in my recovery. During this time, my aunt called to offer encouragement. She advised me "*not to accept the diagnosis I had received*," which turned out to be the best advice she could have given. From that moment on, I decided not to accept it.

Her advice ignited a spark of determination within me. I channeled my energy into applying the strategies and tools provided by the neuropsychologist. This proactive approach transformed my daily routine, fostering a sense of control over my circumstances. It was as if a weight had been lifted, allowing me to see a path forward amidst the chaos.

Rejecting the diagnosis wasn't denying reality but rather refusing to be defined by it. I embraced a mindset of resilience and adaptability, focusing on what I could do rather than what I couldn't. This shift in perspective was instrumental in my recovery journey.

The encouragement and wisdom from my aunt, coupled with the guidance from the neuropsychologist, became a cornerstone of my healing process. Each day, I worked toward regaining a sense of normalcy and stability, redefining my life on my own terms.

Determined to wean myself off the medication prescribed by my neurologist, I drew inspiration from the words of God and the kingdom I represent. It wasn't easy, but I was resolute. In a short time, I succeeded and haven't taken another dose since that day years ago. This journey reinforced the power of faith and self-determination. It taught me how crucial it is to believe in my strength, even when facing seemingly insurmountable challenges. The support from my loved ones and my unwavering faith became my pillars of strength as I navigated this difficult period, emerging stronger and more resilient than ever before.

Not long after, my cousin, an engineer, approached me with an intriguing business proposition. She was uneasy about the idea of me relying entirely on my husband for support, despite his ability to provide. She admired my independence and encouraged me to maintain it. Embracing her proposal, I took a modest loan from her and set to work. Within a year, I had not only repaid the loan but also established a thriving business.

This experience has also given me a deep respect for those battling addiction. I had always been cautious to avoid exposure to addictive substances or behaviors, never wanting to be under such control. However, even the lowest dosage of prescribed medication had altered my brain and significantly impacted my mental health. It was a harrowing experience that opened my eyes to the challenges faced by those struggling with addiction.

Now, I am filled with vitality and free from the shadows of that difficult time. I embrace life with open arms, cherishing each moment because I know how unpredictable it can be. The accident that once seemed like a devastating setback ultimately transformed my life in ways I could never have imagined. It taught me the value of independence and just how powerful faith truly is.

This journey has been a testament to the incredible strength that lies within each of us. The power of faith, self-determination, and the support from loved ones can move mountains, transforming seemingly impossible challenges into opportunities for growth and renewal.

Today, I look back on those challenging times with a sense of gratitude. They were difficult, yes, but they also shaped me into the person I am now. I've learned to appreciate the little victories, celebrate progress, and understand that life's twists and turns can lead to unexpected opportunities. This newfound zest for life serves as a daily reminder that we never know what the next minute, hour, or day will bring. It's a journey of growth, strength, and unyielding spirit—a story of turning trials into triumphs.

In my marriage, we both knew that a divorce was inevitable—our home was never truly a home. While we prayed together, we weren't deeply rooted in God within our married life together. I lacked the daily covering of prayer from the head of the household, and our prayers weren't consistent enough to make a lasting impact as one. The fight within me waned, and I knew this would be the greatest struggle of my life.

Reflecting on this journey, I've come to understand the profound impact of spiritual and emotional grounding in a relationship. The absence of consistent, unified prayer left a void that contributed to our struggles. Realizing this was a pivotal moment, I pushed to find strength and resilience within myself.

The path to growth and healing often involves confronting and embracing our deepest challenges. By turning trials into triumphs, I've discovered a wellspring of inner strength and a newfound appreciation for the unpredictable nature of life. Each setback became an opportunity for growth, each hardship a steppingstone toward a more resilient, empowered self.

Footwork

The inconsistency in our spiritual practices meant that our efforts never truly took root, leaving a void that was impossible to ignore. I felt the weight of the disparity deeply, recognizing that the greatest battle I faced was within our own home.

As we faced the end of our relationship, the idea of remaining friends seemed impossible—we couldn't imagine ever wanting to see each other again. Harsh words were exchanged, lingering in the air, leaving us both in pain, disillusioned, and adrift. But I felt a divine push toward a different approach. The Holy Spirit impressed upon me that this ending needed to be unlike the painful separations I had known before.

Instead of harboring bitterness, I was guided to seek peace and forgiveness. It was a challenging path, but it felt necessary for my own healing and for laying a foundation for future interactions. This spiritual guidance became my anchor, helping me navigate the tumultuous emotions and find a way to part ways with grace.

Embracing this approach required immense strength and faith. It wasn't about forgetting the hurt but about choosing to let go of the anger and resentment that could have consumed us both. By following this divine direction, I aimed to close this chapter of my life with a sense of peace and understanding, rather than leaving it open and festering with unresolved pain.

My first husband accused me of not giving him a second chance, and after dealing with disappointment, neglect, and mistreatment far too many times, my heart put up a "*no vacancy*" sign. Trust… What's that? This time, I knew I needed to switch things up.

Enter accountability. It wasn't just his vices that brought our marriage down; my fiery emotional reactions to his disrespect were part of the problem too. Instead of making a dramatic exit, I stuck around. My words… Oh, they were sharp enough to cut through steel.

So, we tried counseling before hitting the divorce button. Our therapist told us to keep it classy—no low blows. After all, everyone deserves privacy, right? I mean, why stay in a relationship where trust is as rare as a unicorn? There was none.

In the end, we had to say goodbye to our old relationship. Embracing this fresh approach and holding ourselves accountable was like finding a secret cheat code. We broke free from the toxic cycle that had us on lockdown for so long. It was a wild, painful ride, but it led to growth and healing.

This experience taught me the importance of accountability and self-awareness in relationships. It showed me that even in the midst of pain and difficulty, there is always an opportunity for growth and transformation. Embracing this mindset has been key to finding peace and building a stronger, more resilient future.

We learned that keeping the peace and showing respect, even when things get messy, is crucial for real resolution and personal growth. Our divorce journey was a crash course in finding a better path, one that honored the lessons learned and paved the way for a healthier future. Breaking free from the cycle of hurt and mistrust allowed us to discover a more fulfilling way of life and embrace a brighter future with open arms!

I had to understand what was different this time and what God was up to. I truly believe the difference was our three beautiful grandchildren. My ex-husband was their beloved "Papa." Yes, they had a grandfather, whom they absolutely adore, but my husband, despite the challenges in our marriage, never ever treated our grandchildren differently.

We were now beyond the age of parenting new children together, but we shared many fond memories with our grandchildren. I didn't want their bond to end, especially with our oldest grandchild, who had formed a special connection with him. He was less than a year old when my ex and I started dating, and their relationship only grew stronger over time.

It was crucial for me to teach them that you can walk away with grace, respect, and love. Even in the midst of our divorce, we wanted to set an example for them. Our aim was to show that relationships can evolve without losing the core of what makes them special. We wanted to demonstrate that it's possible to handle difficult situations with dignity and compassion, especially for those we love.

So, we walked away as **family**, illustrating that love and respect can persist, even when the nature of the relationship changes. This journey taught us all about the power of resilience and the importance of maintaining bonds, no matter the circumstances.

It was important for our grandchildren to see that even through challenging times, family can remain united in spirit, and the love we have for each other can endure beyond the trials we face. This was the legacy we wanted to leave for them—a testament to the strength of family and the enduring nature of true love and respect.

Embracing this perspective allowed us to model strength and unity for the younger generations. It demonstrated that while relationships may evolve, the core values of love, respect, and support can remain steadfast. Our journey became a powerful example of how to navigate life's challenges with grace and compassion, ensuring that the bonds of family stay strong and meaningful.

Neither of us knew how to navigate through the chaos, so I turned to God for guidance. God said, *"It begins with friendship."* *"Go back to how it first started!"* He instructed. *"Start there,"* The Lord said. *"Focus on the positives, remember the good. After all, if he was so terrible, what does it say about your character for allowing him into your life, let alone marrying him?"*

Exactly, Lord! I thought. *Let's start there.*

When I first met him, he was like a breath of fresh air. Unlike any man I'd ever met, he was easy-going, flowed with the tides, and never complained. His presence was simply refreshing.

That initial connection, built on simplicity and ease, held a special place in my heart. Rediscovering that friendship was like finding a lifeline amidst the chaos. It reminded me of the qualities that had initially drawn me to him and provided a foundation to rebuild from.

Focusing on rekindling that sense of friendship allowed us to approach our challenges from a different perspective. It wasn't about erasing the past but about finding common ground to move forward with understanding and mutual respect. This shift in approach brought a renewed sense of hope and a pathway to healing.

By focusing on those positives and remembering why we first connected, we began to rebuild our relationship on a foundation of friendship and mutual respect. This was how we started to navigate the rough seas, one step at a time, guided by faith and genuine care for one another.

In this new phase, I recalled his easy nature, his refreshing presence, and his ability to flow with the tides without causing a stir. These qualities initially drew me to him and made our relationship feel so effortless.

As we began to reconnect, I focused on letting go of the resentment and cherishing the moments that made me fall in love with him in the first place. It wasn't easy, especially with the painful memories still lingering, but it was necessary for healing for both of us.

We learned to communicate more effectively, express our feelings without resorting to hurtful words, and respect each other's need for privacy. The counselor's advice to avoid low blows and maintain dignity became our guiding principle from our previous sessions.

This process of reconnecting on a deeper level required patience and a commitment to understanding each other better. By prioritizing mutual respect and open communication, we were able to create a new foundation for our relationship, one that was more resilient and meaningful.

I also took accountability for my actions and reactions. While my husband's behavior played a significant role in our struggles, my responses to his actions contributed to the cycle of pain. Recognizing this helped me approach our relationship with a balanced perspective, focusing on solutions rather than blame.

Ultimately, our decision to walk away from our old relationship didn't mean ending our connection. Instead, it was about redefining it to allow us to grow individually. We chose to prioritize *peace, respect,* and *love,* creating a new foundation based on friendship and mutual support.

This journey was a testament to the power of faith, resilience, and the willingness to change. It taught me that even in the face of adversity, it's possible to find a path to healing and growth. By embracing the positives, learning from the past, and trusting in God's guidance, we navigated the challenges and emerged stronger. This newfound perspective transformed our relationship and enriched our lives, allowing us to move forward with a renewed sense of purpose and fulfillment.

We are **one** family! God not only led me to make amends with my most recent husband but also to circle back and make it right with my first husband. He has remarried, and his wife is actively involved in our grandchildren's lives. There's no discord on my part—I wish only the best for them. We've all grown into mature adults who understand the importance of coexistence for the sake of our son and grandchildren while maintaining a friendship. Have we had misunderstandings every now and then? Yes, but nothing to dissolve the work we have put forth.

My grandparents set the ultimate example. I watched my own mother visit her father, my grandfather (R.I.P. Willie Colvin), and his wife, my grandmother (R.I.P. Ethel Colvin). My *bonus* grandmother never treated my mother nor her children as anything other than her own blood. This concept of "*one family*" was instilled in us—whether we realized it at the time or not. It's our family's legacy. "**We are one!**" A legacy of love. One love. There's no such thing as "*step*" or treating anyone as an outsider! I pray that I've made them proud by continuing this family legacy of *God, family, peace*, and *love*.

Witnessing my grandmother's love and care for my grandfather was a profound experience. She was truly remarkable, a testament to strength and compassion. Despite the wounds that many women endure in relationships, she never let those wounds hinder her ability to care for him with steady affection until his final breath.

Having three phenomenal grandmothers was indeed a blessing. Watching her actions was a living lesson in unconditional love and loyalty. Her dedication went beyond the boundaries of their past relationship, showcasing her immense capacity for empathy and kindness. Her legacy continues to inspire me and is a cornerstone of the values we cherish within our family.

Her example instilled in us the importance of treating everyone with love and respect, regardless of the circumstances. This enduring sense of family, rooted in genuine care and compassion, is a legacy I am proud to carry forward and hope to pass on to future generations.

This unity and mutual respect have strengthened my bond with both of my ex-husbands. Being part of our family, they both witnessed this type of love and learned the true meaning of family. We stand together, teaching our grandchildren that love and harmony can prevail, even through life's challenges.

By demonstrating the power of unity and mutual respect, we've shown that it's possible to overcome past difficulties and maintain strong, loving relationships. Our grandchildren can see firsthand the value of family and the importance of supporting one another through thick and thin. This legacy of love and respect is a powerful testament to the enduring strength of family bonds.

Our journey serves as a reminder that, with faith, love, and determination, we can navigate life's challenges and emerge stronger and more connected. It's a beautiful legacy to pass down, ensuring that the values of *God, family, peace,* and *love* continue to thrive in our family for generations to come.

It's "**Not My Fight**" when *God is love.*

The Author

Not My Fight – The Art of Preserving Peace. I am incredibly grateful that fighting has ceased for me in my life. Understanding that not every battle is mine has been transformative! Now I enjoy the beautiful white sand beaches of Florida's west coast and soak in the breathtaking sunsets. Life truly gets better when you don't give up and can envision a brighter future for yourself.

Life has been fulfilling for me already at the age of fifty-two, and it has also given me the chance to help others grow as I have. Each challenge and triumph have shaped me into the person I am today, and I am grateful for every lesson learned along the way.

Through every obstacle, I have gained strength and resilience. Every achievement, no matter how small, has added to my sense of purpose and fulfillment. Reflecting on these experiences has allowed me to appreciate the beauty in life's journey.

In my path, I've met incredible people who have influenced my growth and inspired me to become a better version of myself. Their support and encouragement have been invaluable, and I strive to pay it forward by sharing my knowledge and experiences with others.

As I continue to navigate through life, I look forward to embracing new challenges and opportunities. My journey of self-discovery is ongoing, and I am excited to see what the future holds.

I am committed to using my experiences to inspire and uplift those around me. By sharing my story, I hope to encourage others to persevere and see the potential for growth in every situation. The journey ahead is full of possibilities, and I am ready to face it with gratitude and optimism.

Acknowledgments

This book is dedicated to my most beautiful and gracious grandmother, Ethel Colvin. The impact you have made on my life will forever be felt in how I show up in this world, having had such a bright light guiding me. You are irreplaceable. May your soul rest in peace, and may heaven enjoy the presence of an angel.

To all the brave men and women, to my friends and loved ones who have fought, are still fighting the battle of cancer, and have transitioned on, it is never by our strength alone but by the power *within us* and *surrounding us*.

To my sister, Lisa Figueroa—you are the strongest fighter I have ever encountered. It seems you have faced almost every cancer diagnosis, yet you continue to fight on, refusing to give up. The battle of cancer is relentless, but your spirit is unwavering. They say we shouldn't question God, but I will never understand how someone so loving and caring has had to endure so much pain in life yet still smiles through it all. Thank you for always believing in me. We are *ebony* and *ivory*—my sister from another mother. I've witnessed through you the power of the mind and what we manifest in our lives. It's been a long road, but, my sister, you are forever as beautiful to me as the day we met. You will always be my vibrant, free-spirited *butterfly*.

My Aunt Ruby W., words can't thank you enough for speaking life into me on that day. It literally changed my life. You told me that my story would be my best seller, and I am claiming that it will be. We never know what seeds we are planting, but clearly, you spoke this one into existence. I am forever grateful. I love you!

What can I say, Lo, we did it! It's finally here! I want to extend my heartfelt thanks to Lo B. for listening to God's voice and being an angel during tough times. Your words are an inspiration that the world needs to hear. Writing this book was challenging; it brought back so many memories I wished to leave in the past, but you reassured me time and time again that God had a purpose for this work. You are a true friend. Your beautiful words of encouragement during those toughest days will never be forgotten.

Nalicia S. A., you've been a beacon of inspiration for me over the years, always encouraging and uplifting me, and for that, I am truly humbled. Your constant support and belief in me are treasures I hold close to my heart. I've always believed, "when you know there is a need, one should never have to ask… just do!" And you exemplify that beautifully. Thank you from the bottom of my heart! I love you!

To my photographer, Indra Rogers, I extend my heartfelt thanks for capturing my essence through photography for my latest works. From the moment we met that day in the mall, I sensed a purpose behind our meeting. Since then, our connection has been unwavering, with nothing but positive moments shared. I am thrilled to see what God is doing in your life. Continue to walk in your purpose and enhance lives for the better, capturing all of life's beauty.

To all of my family, loved ones, and friends (social connections), I appreciate your support and encouragement. We all need someone to cheer us along in some capacity, and I am thankful to have such support. To the new connections I have made from coast to coast, your impact has been profound. Witnessing such transparency in this day and age is truly refreshing.

Nadine H., "Nades," my sister—I never felt that I needed a "bestie" until you came along. No matter how hectic your schedule, you always find time to check in on me, and we always find something to laugh about. Whenever we finally link up, it's as if time has stood still. You are the big sister that I never had. You've always sincerely had my best interest at heart, even when we were being stubborn and knuckleheaded. You've made me truly reflect on what it means to be a friend. When I sat still and really grasped our over twenty-year friendship, it is a true reflection of everything that life encompasses; together, *we are a beautiful gift, girl!*

To my ex-husbands, Tony O. and Jordan H., our stories had *ups* and *downs*, but I am grateful for the areas of growth we've experienced. Thank you for planting seeds that have helped me grow into the woman you see today. I appreciate the effort you both have made for us all to get here as a *family. The fight is over, we've won!*

For those who are inspired by this read and wish to explore more of my books, you can visit me online. I hope my work continues to motivate and uplift you. Thank you for being a part of this journey and for your ongoing support!

- *Website:* laowens.com
- *Facebook:* Leandrea Rivers Owens (L.A. Owens)
- *Instagram:* Iamlaowens
- *TikTok:* Iamlaowens